HORSE POWER

Margaret Scariano

A **HIGH ADVENTURE** BOOK
High Noon Books
Novato, California

Cover Design: Jim McConnell
Interior Illustrations: Herb Heidinger

International Standard Book Number: 0-87879-405-0

9 8 7 6 5 4 3 2 1 0
7 6 5 4 3 2 1 0 9 8

High Noon Books

a division of ATP
20 Commercial Blvd.
Novato, California 94949

Contents

Chapter 1

Fired!

The manager's words came as a shock to Rob. "Okay, Talbot. I've had it with you. This is the third time you've been told to finish that job. You're fired."

"I was going to do it right after lunch," Rob said to the grocery store manager. "And I was all done except for putting the canned soup on the shelves."

"So nobody's supposed to buy soup until you get ready to do your job? Forget it. I need someone I can depend on. Pick up your check at the office." The manager walked away.

Rob stood outside the grocery store. He looked at the check in his hand. Two weeks pay! At least his rent was paid. But his car payment was due. He had to pay that or he would lose his car. Without his car he might as well hang it up as far as Susan Hall went. She liked to go places, and where could you go without a car?

Rob kicked the curb. He just had to get a job — and soon. He walked into the pool hall. A lot of the guys hung out there. Maybe someone there knew of a job.

"Hi, guy," Johnny Bates called. He chalked the end of his cue stick. "You have the day off?"

"You might say that." Rob tried to smile. "I was fired."

"Tough luck, Rob. What are you going to do now?"

"I was hoping one of you guys might know of a job," Rob answered.

"Are you kidding?" Chuck Fuller reached in a bag for another pretzel. "If I knew of a job, I'd take it myself."

Weasel Worden lined up the eight ball. "I heard they're looking for a couple of guys to carry mail," he said.

"A postman's job?" Rob asked.

"How do I know?" Weasel aimed at the eight ball. "Check over at the Last Chance Restaurant." The ball spun across the felt into the side pocket of the pool table.

"Good shot, Weasel," Rob said. "And thanks for the tip. I'll check it out right away." He walked to the door. "See you guys later."

Rob hurried down the street to the Last Chance Restaurant. In his mind he saw himself driving a mail jeep. A jeep wasn't his choice of cars but he needed the job. Maybe he could fix the mail jeep up. Put some stripes on it or a fancy bumper.

At the lunch counter Rob asked the waitress, "Is there someone here hiring mail men?"

She smiled at him. "See that man wearing the cowboy hat at the round table over there? He's the one you should see. Go on over."

Rob looked at the man with the big hat shoved to the back of his head. He was talking to a dark-haired man. Was that man after the mail job, too? Rob started toward the table. Should he interrupt? He didn't want someone to beat him out of a job. The man with the cowboy hat might think there were no other guys wanting work. He decided he would stand beside the table. That way the man would know he wanted to talk with him.

In a few minutes Rob heard the dark-haired man say he didn't want the job. Rob's heart beat fast. Maybe he had a chance. Then his car payment worries would be over. And he and Susan would still have wheels.

He watched the dark-haired man walk away.

3

*Rob looked at the man with the big hat
shoved to the back of his head.*

He stepped up to the round table. "Sir, I heard
you were hiring mail men."

"Well, at least, you're the right size," the man
with the cowboy hat said.

Right size, Rob thought. He'd always felt he
was on the small side. But he was strong. He kept
himself in pretty good shape.

4

The man stood up and stuck out his hand. "My name is Handley. Hal Handley."

"Rob Talbot." They shook hands.

"Sit down, Rob, and I'll tell you about the job. Did you ever hear about the Pony Express?"

"That was a bunch of guys who carried mail during the gold rush days. About 100 years ago. Right?" Rob asked.

"Yes. The Pony Express was a mail service between St. Joseph, Missouri, and Sacramento, California. That's a distance of 1,838 miles. Riders rode fast horses. Each rider would carry the mail so many miles. When a rider reached his home station, he'd give the mail to another rider to carry to the next station. Do you understand?" Hal Handley looked at Rob closely.

"Yes. Sure. Kind of like a relay race."

"Right. The Pony Express service was a relay of riders who carried the mail almost 2,000 miles. And it only took them ten days."

Rob tried to pay attention. What had all this history to do with carrying the mail today?

Mr. Handley was still talking. "Today we need Pony Express riders again. A huge mudslide has blocked Highway 50 in the northern part of the state. Towns are completely cut off from mail service. The only way to get to these towns is by horse." Mr. Handley jabbed at Rob's upper arm. "And that's where you come in, my man."

"Me?" The thought of riding a horse caused cold sweat to break out on Rob's forehead.

"Interested?" Mr. Handley asked. "You're about the right size—not too heavy to be a load for the horse on a long ride."

The mail might have to be delivered, Rob thought. But not by him on a horse! No wonder the dark-haired man had walked away. Rob pushed his chair back and stood.

"Thanks, Mr. Handley. Let me think about it." He *would* think about it. Right up until the mudslide was cleared. He turned to walk away.

Just then, out of the corner of his eye he saw Susan. She was sitting in a booth having coffee with Wes Zimmer.

He turned back to Mr. Handley. "I've thought about it, Sir. I'd like the job as Pony Express rider."

Chapter 2

Hired!

Mr. Handley stood up. "That's great, Rob. Just sit right down here. I'll get you an application form." He reached down to a briefcase beside his chair. "Fill this out and you're hired."

Quickly Rob filled in his name, age, address, education, and last job. When he came to the part about horseback riding experience, he stopped. He remembered when he was a kid. He had ridden a pony at a carnival. The pony was connected to a long rope on a pole. Rob remembered going round and round the dirt circle. Did that count as riding experience? Then there were the horses on the merry-go-round. He'd spend a lot of time on them!

Rob looked up at Mr. Handley. Should he tell him he didn't know too much about riding? Just then he heard Susan laugh. He looked at her and Wes in the booth. No. He wouldn't tell. He needed this job. Besides, what could be hard about sitting on a horse? It was the same as a pony, wasn't it? Just bigger, that's all. He handed Mr. Handley the application form.

Mr. Handley looked it over. "Fine, Rob. You'll do fine. And you're not too big. That's good. Makes it easier on the horse." He told Rob about the pay and his day off on Sunday. Then he said, "You get your gear together right away. I'll tell our man at Folger Flat that you'll be up there tomorrow. Okay?"

"Yes, Mr. Handley. I'll drive up in the morning." Rob shook hands. "Thanks for the job. I need it."

"You'll earn every cent you make, Rob. Pony Express riding isn't easy, even today."

Susan was standing near the cash register when Rob walked out. He stopped. "Hi, didn't expect to see you here."

Susan laughed. "And I didn't expect to see you. How come you're not working?"

Rob didn't want to tell her he'd been fired. But he didn't want to lie either. Before he could think of something to say, Susan said, "Don't tell me. You've been fired! What happened?"

"The store manager got mad. He said I didn't finish putting the canned soup on the shelves."

Rob looked at Susan. She looked unhappy. "But guess what? I'm going to be a Pony Express rider. Carry the mail. My day off is Sunday. So how about spending it with me? We could take a picnic to the beach or the park."

"Sure, Rob. I'd like that," Susan said. Then Wes came up and took her arm.

"Ready, Susan? See you around, Rob." Wes led Susan to the door.

"Sunday?" Rob called to Susan.

"Right, pony boy." She stopped at the door and turned around. "Hey, Rob, one thing about this new job—you'll have to finish it. Otherwise, you'll be in the middle of nowhere." She laughed.

Rob didn't think it was too funny. And he didn't like the way Wes held onto her arm. Well, just wait until he came back on Sunday. He'd show her he wasn't a quitter. He'd have money for his car payment and a trip to the beach.

Rob walked back to the pool hall to tell the guys about his job. Weasel Worden laughed so hard, tears came to his eyes.

"You? A Pony Express rider?" Weasel, still laughing, leaned against the wall.

"What's so funny? You're the one who told me about the job. Now you're laughing." Rob began to feel angry. Weasel always made him feel like

9

two cents.

Finally Weasel stopped laughing long enough to tell him, "Just think about it, Rob. Pony Express rider. The only horse you know is a "charlie" horse. That's when you get a terrible cramp in your leg. And express? That means fast. The only fast thing you do is eat." Weasel

"You? A Pony Express rider?"
said Weasel, still laughing.

started laughing again. "And rider? Rob, without the eyes you wouldn't know the front from the back of a horse. How are you going to sit on a horse?"

"Aw, back off, Weasel," Chuck Fuller said. "Give him a break."

"He can get that on his own," Weasel answered. "Okay. Okay. Enough's enough. I'll stop making fun of you." He waved to Rob and Chuck to follow him to a booth. They ordered hamburgers from the waitress. Then Weasel took out a notebook and pencil. "I grew up on a ranch. I know about horses. Here's what you need to ride the trail." He started writing.

Rob looked at the list. "Boots! I was going to wear my tennis shoes."

"No way, Rob," Weasel said. "That would be dangerous."

"Aw, come on. I can't afford boots. Besides, this job just lasts until Highway 50 is open again. I'm not taking the job for the rest of my life."

"You said the magic word, Rob. Life. Cowboy boots with a heel keep your foot from slipping through the stirrup. Then if the horse throws you, he won't drag you. I've seen people get badly hurt that way."

Rob's throat felt dry. What had he gotten

himself into?

Weasel kept talking. "Don't worry about the boots. My brother's will fit you."

They went on down the list — boots, hat, kerchief, warm jacket, rain poncho, and gloves. Finally, Rob was set.

"I just hope the horse likes how I look," Rob said with a laugh. "Thanks, guys." His voice trembled. He was glad they didn't seem to notice how up-tight he really was.

The next morning he drove to Folger Flat. Mr. Handley had told him to go to a rooming house and get a room first. Then he was to go to the Pony Express office. It was next to the blacksmith's shop.

Folger Flat was a small town. Rob left his car in front of the rooming house and walked a block down the street to the Pony Express office. He knocked on the office door.

"Ain't locked. Come on in," someone yelled.

Rob stepped inside a small room. A tall, thin man came to the counter. "You must be the new guy Hal Handley called me about."

"Yes, sir."

"I'm Jim-Bob, the boss of this here outfit. I've been carrying the mail myself the last three days. Fellow before you couldn't take it. Just quit. Left me to deliver mail and run the office. Sure glad you're here. Follow me. I'll introduce you to Smiley."

Rob followed the man out the back door to a corral and barn. All the time Jim-Bob was talking. "You'll ride a five-mile stretch. You go as far as Miles End. Give your mail pouch to the next rider. He will carry it five miles farther. You take his mail and bring it back here to be sent to other parts of the country. Your home station is here at Folger Flat. Pay you each Saturday. No work on Sunday. But you'd better be on time Monday morning or else." He slid the barn door open and walked to a stall. "Well, son, how do you like him?"

Rob looked over the railing. Cripes! The horse was as big as an elephant!

"This here is Smiley. Come on, Smiley. Show Rob your nice smile."

The horse pulled up his lip showing a row of large, yellow teeth.

Sweat broke out on Rob's forehead but his feet were cold. His teeth chattered. He looked over the railing of the stall again. Smiley sure didn't look like any merry-go-round horse he'd ever seen.

Chapter 3

Scared Stiff

In his room at the rooming house Rob lay on the bed. After Jim-Bob had finished telling him about being a Pony Express rider, he said, "You'll start tomorrow, Rob. Get yourself an early supper and a good night's rest. And be here tomorrow morning at 7:00 sharp. That'll give me time to go over the route with you. And give you plenty of time to saddle Smiley. Get him used to you."

The words "Get him used to you" went round and round in Rob's head. What was there to get used to? Did the horse like some guys and not others? Cripes! He wasn't looking for a horse friend. He just wanted to get from Folger Flat to Miles End with the mail. He turned over on his side and rolled up the pillow under his head. He closed his eyes and tried to think of Susan. But instead he saw Smiley's big, yellow teeth.

He turned the light on and looked at the clock. Eleven-thirty. He had to get some sleep.

That night he dreamed about a merry-go-round. In his dream he heard the sound of the music. He could hardly wait for it to stop so he could get on. But when he ran to find a horse, they all were brown with black tails. A merry-go-round and all the horses were Smileys!

The alarm went off the next morning at 6:00. Rob felt as if he'd just started to sleep. He tried to hurry. He wanted to be on time. But first he had to wait his turn to shower. Then, his landlady made him eat breakfast. She was a good cook, but she was sure slow. Finally he hurried out the door down the street. But he wasn't used to walking in cowboy boots. The boot on his left foot rubbed. At ten minutes after seven he limped into the Pony Express office.

The office was empty. Rob walked out to the corral and barn. Smiley was saddled and tied to the hitching post. Jim-Bob stood at the horse's side with a large, leather pouch in his hand.

"I'm here, Jim-Bob," Rob called out.

"So I see. You're late. When I say seven, I mean exactly seven—just that. The mail must be delivered on time. Other men are waiting at their stations to do their job. It's not fair to make them wait." Jim-Bob set the pouch on the ground. He raised the stirrup over the saddle horn. With a grunt he made the cinch tight.

Rob could see the frown on Jim-Bob's face. He bet that Jim-Bob had thought he was not going to show up. Then Jim-Bob would have to deliver the mail. Rob walked over to the hitching rail.

"Sorry, I'm late. It won't happen again."

Jim-Bob just nodded. "All right, then, take this leather pouch. It's filled with mail. And it's valuable. Tie it to your saddle with these straps."

Rob looked at the big, brown bag. It had large flaps with pockets that could be locked. Rob tied it to his saddle. His hands shook. He wondered if he looked as scared as he felt. Maybe he should just admit he'd never ridden anything wilder than a pony at a carnival. Just quit and get out of there.

"Rob, didn't mean to jump you the first thing in the morning." Jim-Bob leaned against the corral. "I figured you weren't coming. Another quitter. Sorry."

"That's all right. I understand." How could he walk off now? He finished tying the mail pouch. Then he stepped back. Smiley looked as if he'd grown a foot bigger during the night.

"Study this map, Rob. Then put it in your pocket. It shows the route you will take and all the landmarks. You know — like the saw mill and the wooden bridge and the old shack. You shouldn't have any trouble."

Rob looked at the home-made map. He found Folger Flat and followed the wiggly line to Miles End. It sure didn't look far. Just a couple of turns and he'd be there.

"Well, better get going. You should reach Miles End no later than 10:00 this morning. Swap mail pouches with the other rider. Then get yourself something to eat. Head back to Folger Flat around 1:00. That way the mail can go out from here on the five o'clock truck."

"Is this the time I will always leave?" Rob asked.

"No, just the first morning. These past two days I got on the trail at 8:00. Gave me plenty of time." Jim-Bob untied Smiley. He held the rein close to Smiley's mouth. "Mount up, Rob."

Rob stepped up to the left side of the horse. Smiley moved away. Rob grabbed the reins in one hand and put the toe of his boot in the stirrup. With his other hand he grabbed the saddle horn. He felt Jim-Bob watching him. Could he possibly swing his right leg over the saddle? With a slight bounce he tried. He made it! He was really sitting tall in the saddle. The ground looked very far down.

Jim-Bob let go of the rein. "You're on your way, Rob. Good luck!" He slapped Smiley's rump. The horse broke into a trot.

Rob bounced down the trail toward the woods. He couldn't believe he was really riding.

Then he heard Jim-Bob yell, "Remember. No matter what happens, the mail must go through!"

Rob bobbed his head in answer. He didn't dare let go of the saddle horn.

Chapter 4

The Tenderfoot

Now the forest was all around Rob. Almost no
sunlight came through the tall trees. It was dim
and dark and silent. The rains had made the trail
slippery in places. There were muddy prints from
many hooves on the path. On both sides of the
trail were large drifts of snow. Some of them
looked as big as a house. In other places huge
rocks stood close to the trail. Rob couldn't help
shivering. Even the extra heavy jacket didn't
warm the chill of fear inside him.

He wondered if he should stop and study the
map. But what if he couldn't get Smiley started
again? Besides, the horse seemed to know the
way.

Rob looked around. Even if he had wanted to
quit and go back, there wasn't room enough on
the trail to back up. Just go forward. Farther and
farther into the dark forest.

Smiley's trot was as rough as a car with no shocks. Rob bounced up and down. Every part of him jiggled. Rob thought about his car and Susan. At least, now with a pay check he'd be able to keep his car and take Susan to nice places.

Suddenly Smiley slowed down. Rob looked around. What was wrong? Then down the trail a few feet he saw a fallen tree. It blocked the path. Now what was he going to do? He couldn't turn around. He sure hoped Smiley wasn't planning to jump it!

Smiley slowed to a walk. At the tree the horse turned and with short leaps climbed the hill. He carefully stepped over the snowy ground until he was beyond the tree. Then he made his way down the hill to the trail again.

Rob let out his breath. "We did it, Smiley! We did it!" Without thinking he patted Smiley's neck. Smiley began to trot again. Rob groaned. The inside part of his legs felt raw.

Now he could see the river below. Melting snow had filled it. The noisy water roared along the river bed. Then he saw the old saw mill. A landmark. So they were still heading the right way. But that river. So close. So swift. Rob wished Smiley would slow down. No way did he want them to slip and tumble into that wild river.

But Smiley trotted on. The trail followed the side of the mountain. It dropped down close to the river. It wound through trees and across a wooden bridge. Smiley's hooves sounded loud on the planks.

The trail cut through a meadow. They passed an old shack with a sod roof. Another landmark. Then they were in the woods again. Finally, they came out of the forest. There was Miles End. They'd made it!

Smiley trotted down the main street of the town. Rob looked for the Pony Express office. But Smiley seemed to know exactly where to go. He stopped at the hitching rail in front of the Pony Express office.

Rob sat there a moment. He didn't know whether he could lift his leg to get off the horse. He took a deep breath and swung his leg over the saddle. It was all he could do not to moan. Slowly he put his foot on the ground. Then he removed the other foot from the stirrup. He held onto the edges of the saddle blanket. His legs felt shaky. His whole body was stiff and sore.

Well, he couldn't stand there forever. He took a deep breath and then a step. He grabbed hold of the hitching post. Every muscle in his legs hurt. He looped the reins over the hitching rail.

Slowly he stepped around Smiley to get the mail pouch. His fingers were stiff, too, from gripping the reins. He fumbled with the straps holding the mail bag. Finally he got the straps untied and carried the mail into the office.

He laid the pouch on the counter. Two men sat at the back of the room. One of them was the postmaster. The other one said, "Hey, you the new man?"

"If you mean Pony Express man, yes."

"You're about twenty minutes early. Great! It'll give me an early start on my trip." The man stood up and walked to the counter. He stuck out his hand. "I'm Windy. Windy Waters. I take the next five miles with the mail." He leaned down behind the counter. "Here's the mail for you to take back to Folger Flat." He slid a mail bag across the counter. "What did you say your name was?"

The postmaster laughed. "You can see now where he got the nickname of Windy."

Rob smiled. "Rob Talbot," he said to Windy. Then he asked, "Where's a good place to eat?"

"Mac's General Store. It's right next door. They have a little lunch counter. And everything else from pins to motors," Windy said.

The postmaster said, "Hey, Windy, put Rob's

return mail under the counter. He doesn't want to have to carry it around with him."

"Sure thing." Windy slid the bag beneath the counter again. "Well, I'm on my way." He picked up his bag of mail and headed for the door. "You know the old saying, 'Neither snow, nor rain, nor heat, will keep me from that saddle seat.' "

The man in the back yelled, "Git on with you, Windy. As usual, you're full of hot air."

"I'll be back in a little while for the return mail," Rob said.

With a kind of salute the postmaster said, "Sure thing."

Rob moved his sore body carefully toward Mac's General Store. One moment he thought he'd like to sit down. The next moment he knew he'd never sit again. What would it be like to go through life either standing or lying down?

At the lunch counter he ordered steak and eggs. No point in hurting on an empty stomach.

"Want some coffee, too, tenderfoot?" the clerk asked.

Rob nodded, then asked, "Tenderfoot?"

"Means someone who ain't done much riding." The clerk filled a mug with coffee.

Rob laughed. "It sure isn't my feet that are tender!"

23

"Best thing is to get right back on that horse and ride for an hour or so. Take the soreness right out."

All the way back to Folger Flat, Rob tried to believe that. But it was all he could do to sit in the saddle and hope Smiley knew the way home. Each step Smiley took shook him clear down to his toes. Why didn't someone think to pad a saddle? And his legs—from the knees up—must be raw. His jeans rubbed as if there were sand on them. He could hardly wait to get back to the rooming house. He closed his eyes. He thought about how good a hot bath would feel.

To keep his mind off his pain, he planned what he would do. First, he'd drop the mail and Smiley off at the Pony Express office. Then he'd limp to the rooming house. After his bath he'd stretch out on his bed until supper time. And tonight maybe he'd just lie on the bed and read.

But Jim-Bob greeted him at the corral. Rob climbed off Smiley and handed the mail pouch to him. "Well, guess I'll head over to the rooming house, Jim-Bob."

"Whoa, there, Rob. How about Smiley? Ain't you going to take care of him?"

Rob's hopes of a hot bath sank into his boots. "What do I have to do?"

Jim-Bob showed him how to take off the saddle and bridle. He put a halter on the horse. Then he gave Rob a brush. "Go to it, Rob. Smiley deserves a good brushing. A good rider takes care of his horse."

Jim-Bob watched as Rob brushed. "Now, Rob, take Smiley to the trough for water. Then grab that can and dish up some oats to put in his feed bag."

Rob finally finished caring for Smiley. He followed Jim-Bob to the office.

At the door to the office Jim-Bob turned. He slapped Rob on the back. "Most days the riders help sort the next day's mail. But you look beat. Get on home now and get a good night's rest. See you in the morning."

"Thanks, Jim-Bob." Rob limped up the street to the rooming house.

Trouble on the Trail

The next two days went smoothly. Even Rob's saddle soreness was gone. Rob was beginning to enjoy the ride on Smiley. They were a team. Rob now knew the route almost as well as the horse did.

He enjoyed the stories he heard about the first Pony Express riders. They really had it tough. Their routes were longer. Indians attacked them. The pay was low.

When Rob woke up on Saturday, his fourth day, it was raining. He jumped out of bed and hurried to get ready. It would be a slower ride today. He'd have to start earlier. After all, he couldn't keep the next rider waiting. Rob smiled as he thought of Windy Waters. He was a talker!

At the barn Jim-Bob warned him about the trail. "Smiley's a good strong horse, Rob, but don't rush him. That trail is going to be slick.

You best get going. But take it easy, son."

"I will, Jim-Bob." Rob checked to be sure the mail pouch was protected from the rain.

Then Jim-Bob handed him a small package. "Tuck this inside your poncho. It isn't mail. It's medicine. The doctor sent word on the short wave radio that he needed it. Some kid is real sick at Miles End. Drop it off at Mac's General Store. The doctor will pick it up there."

Rob tucked the package inside his shirt. "Right. See you this afternoon, Jim-Bob." He and Smiley started for the trail through the woods.

Today with no sun coming through the trees at all, the forest seemed darker than ever. Smiley didn't trot today. He seemed to know that the trail was slick and muddy.

They finally reached the place where the trail ran 30 or 40 feet above the river. Rob never liked this part of the trip. That river looked so wild and cold. One slip on Smiley's part and they'd be in it. Several times Smiley stumbled and Rob's heart pounded. He'd be glad to get away from the river. The trail climbed up a slight slope. Smiley stopped. Rob gasped. The trail was gone. Instead mud oozed down the mountain side into the wild river below.

Smiley stopped. Rob gasped. The trail was gone!

Thunder like a drum roll rumbled through the canyon. Lightning flashed in the sky. Smiley jumped in fright. Rob grabbed the saddle horn to keep from falling off. I'd better calm Smiley, he thought. This is no place to be jumping around.

"Easy, boy." Rob stroked Smiley's neck. "Easy does it." The words squeezed out from Rob's tight throat. Now Smiley stood stiffly still.

Rob tried to keep calm. Figure out what to do. With no trail maybe he'd have to turn back. Not finish the route today. Nobody in his right mind would try to cross that sea of mud. Besides, I'm a mailman—a Pony Express rider—not a dare devil. He looked about to see where he could turn Smiley around to head back to Folger Flat. He looked over his shoulder to the trail behind him. Something scratched his chest. Then he remembered. The medicine for the sick child.

Big deal, he thought. There's no way I'm going to risk a fall into that river. Then he thought, what if the child dies because I don't deliver—don't finish the job?

Chapter 6

Dead End and Danger

Rob hadn't been afraid since the first day. But he was afraid now. He knew he'd have to try something. He couldn't just stay there and wait. He studied the land below the washed-out trail. That was no good. The mud was flowing right into the river. There was no room for Smiley and him to get past. They would get stuck in the mud for sure. Then Rob searched above the trail for a way to get through the trees. It wasn't a great plan but it was worth a try. Maybe they could make it through the forest. Later they could get back on the trail.

"Come on, Smiley." Rob reined the horse toward the hillside. But Smiley wouldn't move. "You did it before. Leaped right up the side of the hill to get around the fallen tree. Remember? You can do it, Smiley." Rob made a clicking noise with his mouth. Finally Smiley gave a couple of short leaps, and they were above the washed-out trail.

The horse made his way carefully over snags and brush. The rain had melted some of the snow. But now the ground was slippery with pine needles. Sometimes huge rocks blocked their way. They were moving very slowly. Weaving in and out of the trees took time. Sometimes the branches scratched Rob's face or back. But at least they were going toward Miles End with the medicine and the mail!

Suddenly Rob felt Smiley grow stiff. Then he gave a fearful snort. Almost at the same time Rob saw the mountain lion. It was crouched on the rock just above them. The lion snarled. Its teeth looked sharp.

The hairs on the back of Rob's neck stood up. Should he yell and try to scare the lion off? Or duck down low on the horse and hope the lion would jump over him? Before he could decide, the lion snarled again. Then he sprang.

Smiley leaped forward and bounded through the forest. Rob grabbed hold of the saddle horn. He held on for dear life. Smiley laid his ears back. He stretched his neck out. He panted. He dodged around huge rocks. He jumped over fallen trees. Once he stumbled. That's it, Rob thought, we're going down. But the horse didn't fall.

Rob ducked low branches and hung on. Was the mountain lion gaining? Could it outrun a horse? On the one hand, Rob wished Smiley would stop. But if he did, then what? How could he defend himself and Smiley against a wild animal? Rob bent down close to Smiley's neck. He closed his eyes and hoped for the best.

It seemed hours before Smiley suddenly stopped. Rob opened his eyes. A canyon wall was in front of him. He looked behind him. No mountain lion closing in for the kill. But now what?

The forest was quiet. It had stopped raining. The only sound was Smiley's breathing — short, tired pants. Rob patted his neck. He was sweaty. "You did fine, Smiley." Rob talked softly to the frightened horse. "Catch your breath. I've got to figure out where we are."

It helped to talk out loud. Somehow then Rob didn't feel quite so alone. He looked around. Everything looked strange. Had they gone that far from the trail? He tried to keep calm. To think clearly. Not panic. But he kept looking over his shoulder. Was the mountain lion following them? Just waiting for its chance to spring?

Smiley's breathing was normal now. Rob wished his was. His heart was pounding hard. His hands were sweaty. And he had a sick feeling deep inside. There was no way around that canyon wall. It was a dead end.

Chapter 7

Lost and Late

Rob shook his head. Just his luck. The one time he really felt he should finish the job, he couldn't. A canyon wall had stopped him. But that wasn't all.

He was not only at a dead end, but he was lost! There were no landmarks. He and Smiley had passed the saw mill. They had crossed over the wooden bridge. He should be able to see the old shack in the meadow. But all he saw was the canyon wall in front of him and trees all around.

He swallowed hard. His throat was dry with fear again. He glanced down at his chest. He could almost see each beat of his heart. Smiley shook his head. Rob patted his neck. "You're as puzzled as I am, aren't you, old boy?"

One thing for sure. That wall wasn't going to go away. He'd have to find another way. He tried to remember what to do when lost. First thing was to keep calm. Rob took a deep breath to clear his mind. Then, he looked around for something — anything — that he might have seen before. He almost laughed out loud. Every tree looked the same to him. "Oh, cripes!" he moaned. "What now?" A dead end is a dead end whether at a street in the city or a canyon in the mountains. Maybe he should just turn around. Try to go back to the mud slide on the trail.

But he couldn't do that. The mountain lion might still be there. Just thinking about its snarl and sharp teeth made Rob shiver.

Then he remembered the river. If he listened for its sound, he could walk in that direction. Once he found the river, he could follow it to Miles End.

He pointed Smiley down the mountain side. They went at an angle because it was so steep. The last thing he needed was for Smiley to slip. It was a jerky ride. Several times Smiley's legs seemed to give out. He'd stumble. And Rob's heart would almost stop.

Rob heard the roar of the river below them. Finally he saw it. They were going to make it! All he had to do was follow the river to Miles End.

But when they reached level ground near the river, Rob had another problem. Smiley's jerky walk was due not only to the steep mountain. His front leg had been hurt.

Rob got off the horse. He led Smiley close to the river. He took his handkerchief from his pocket and wet it in the cold water. Then he bathed Smiley's leg with it. Smiley shuffled his hooves about. "It's all right." Rob patted the

Then he bathed Smiley's leg with it.

horse. "Cold is good for sprains." Smiley turned his head toward Rob. The horse pulled his lip back, showing his big, yellow teeth. This time it looked like a real smile. Rob made several trips to the river to wet the handkerchief.

Then he led Smiley a few steps. The horse limped. Rob knew he couldn't ride him any farther. He'd have to walk the rest of the way to Miles End. Windy Waters would be waiting for the mail. Then he thought about the small package inside his shirt. Medicine for a sick child. He had to get going.

But what should he do about Smiley? He could tie him to a tree. Deliver the mail. Then come back and walk him slowly into Miles End. But then he thought about the mountain lion. What if it came back and Smiley couldn't get away? He couldn't leave him. They started the trip together. They would finish it together.

Rob picked up the reins. He led the horse along the river bank toward town. The going was rough. It was slow. Each time Rob looked back to see how Smiley was doing, the horse seemed to smile.

The river flowed through the meadow. Rob saw the old shack. At least, they were going in the right direction. Finally, he was on the edge of

Miles End. He knew he was long over-due. Would he get fired?

He led Smiley down the main street to the Pony Express office. In a way he was glad Smiley couldn't walk fast. Rob hated to face the postmaster. Then he thought about the medicine. He hoped he was in time for the sick child.

He tied Smiley at the hitching post in front of the Pony Express office. He untied the mail bag from the saddle. First, he'd drop the medicine off at Mac's General Store next to the Pony Express office. Then he'd deliver the mail—and maybe get fired!

Chapter 8

A Job Well Done!

Rob hurried into Mac's General Store with the small package in one hand and the mail bag in the other.

"Here's the medicine the doctor asked for," he said to the clerk. He set the package on the counter.

The clerk looked at him. His eyes grew wide. "You the Pony Express rider from Folger Flat?"

"Yeah. You know me. I've been in here the past three days for lunch."

Then the clerk reached across the counter. He grabbed Rob's hand and shook it. "You made it! When you didn't show up, we thought you were dead!"

Rob looked up at the clock on the wall. He was three hours late. But he was far from dead.

"What happened? How did you get here?" the clerk asked excitedly.

"I can't talk to you now. Have to get this mail to the Pony Express office. See you at lunch." Rob hurried from the store.

When he walked in the office, the postmaster acted just like the store clerk. He jumped up from his desk and hurried to the counter. "You made it, Rob." He grabbed Rob's hand and shook it. Then he pounded him on the back. He turned and called, "Hey, Windy, the tenderfoot made it!"

Windy Waters walked out of the back room. "Just talking with Jim-Bob. It's a good thing the telephones are working again. He's called three times in the last hour and a half. He sure was worried about you." Windy jabbed Rob in the upper part of his arm. "Good job, Rob. I better do mine now." He picked up Rob's mail bag and shoved the return mail toward Rob. He waved. "See you later, guys. I got to get this mail on its way."

The postmaster pointed to a chair by his desk. "Sit down, Rob. Take a load off your feet. Sure glad to see you're all right. When you didn't get here at the usual time, we thought you got buried in the mudslide," the postmaster said.

"There was a mudslide on the trail. Smiley and I climbed above it."

"Not that one."

"Hey, Windy, the tenderfoot made it!"

"Another one?" Rob thought he must have missed it because he had followed the river.

"Yeah. Another one. Took out the bridge this time." The postmaster looked over at Rob and grinned. "How are you on swimming?"

Rob laughed. "Just about as good as I was on riding!"

The postmaster slapped him on the back. "By George, who says they don't make 'em like they used to? You did all right. You finished the job."

The kind words felt like the warm sun on Rob's face. A bridge out seemed like nothing after the fear of the last four hours. He felt good. Then a new thought chilled him.

How was he going to get back to Folger Flat with the mail? And if he couldn't get back to Folger Flat today, how was he going to see Susan tomorrow on Sunday?

Rob sighed. At least he hadn't been fired. And he hadn't quit. He felt good about himself.

The phone rang. The postmaster answered it. Then he handed it to Rob. "It's Jim-Bob."

Jim-Bob told Rob what a great job he had done. Then Rob told him about Smiley's lame leg. "The bridge is out and I don't have a horse. Any ideas, Jim-Bob?"

Jim-Bob told him to get a horse from the postmaster. Also, there was another route he could take to get back to Folger Flat. "It's a little longer, Rob, but it's safe. Get a map from the office. See you late this afternoon."

"But, Jim-Bob, what about the bridge? How long will it be out?" Rob asked.

"We're putting together a crew right now to

work on it. The foreman says he's sure they can put together a temporary bridge tomorrow. That is, if he can get enough workers."

"I'll help," Rob said. Then he remembered his date with Susan.

"Great, Rob. I knew I could count on you."

Before Rob left for Folger Flat, he called Susan long distance.

"Oh, Rob, it's you. I hope you didn't get fired again."

"No. The fact is I'm going to have to work tomorrow to build a bridge." Rob told her about the mudslides.

For a few moments Susan didn't speak. Rob's spirits sagged. He'd lost her. She didn't care about Pony Express or mudslides or rebuilding bridges. All she cared about was fun. He hadn't thought Susan was that kind of girl.

Then she said, "I understand, Rob. But will you be able to see me next Sunday?" Her voice was low.

Now Rob was grinning from ear to ear. "Sure, Susan. I'd be there tomorrow but I've got a job to finish."

"I know. I can hardly wait to see you. I want to hear all about your work. See you next Sunday, OK?"

"You bet," Rob answered. His heart pounded—not in fear this time, but with joy.

"Where's that mail bag?" he called. "I'm on my way!"